My
Adorable

Fox

For Mum, I'm so glad I got
your creative genes! S.H.

Scholastic Children's Books

An imprint of Scholastic Ltd
Euston House, 24 Eversholt Street, London, NW1 1DB, UK
Registered office: Westfield Road, Southam, Warwickshire, CV47 0RA
SCHOLASTIC and associated logos are trademarks and/or
registered trademarks of Scholastic Inc.

First published in the UK by Scholastic Ltd, 2016

Text copyright © Scholastic Ltd, 2016

ISBN 978 1407 16249 2

A CIP catalogue record for this book
is available from the British Library.

Printed by CPI Group (UK) Ltd, Croydon, CR0 4YY
Papers used by Scholastic Children's Books are made
from wood grown in sustainable forests.

1 3 5 7 9 10 8 6 4 2

www.scholastic.co.uk

My
Adorable

Fox

Sarah Hawkins

SCHOLASTIC

1

The tear rolled down Mia's cheek and dripped off her nose. She hugged her old toy tiger closer and squeezed him tight.

The door creaked open, spilling light into the room.

"Oh, Mia," Dad said as he saw her sitting up in bed. "Still upset?"

She nodded and Dad came and sat on the bed next to her. "I know you had a tough day at school but, darling, all friends have arguments sometimes. Even adults. Even Mum and I have fights, but that doesn't mean we don't love each other."

Mia shook her head. Dad didn't

understand. Emily was her best friend – except now she seemed to like someone else better. When the new girl, Zara, had come to school, their teacher had asked Mia and Emily to show her around. At first it had been fun. But now Emily was spending more time with Zara than Mia! Today they'd had to work in pairs during a drama lesson and Zara and Emily had gone together. Mia had got cross and she and Emily had had a huge fight. Worst of all, for the next two weeks it was the Easter holidays. She and Emily normally saw each other lots over the holidays, but now Mia didn't know if they would. She didn't even know if they were friends any more.

"But she's my best friend," she croaked.

"I'm sure she still is." Dad kissed the top of her head. "Now, come on, lie down and go to sleep. It's getting late."

Mia hugged Tiger and climbed under the blankets.

"I'll come and check on you in a bit," Dad promised. "But shut your eyes and try to stop thinking about it. It will all seem better in the morning."

Mia nodded, and Dad went out, swinging the door shut so that all she could see was a line of light around the edge.

Mia snuggled down and closed her eyes. She'd cried so much that they felt puffy and gritty, like they had sand in them. She tried to go to sleep, but as she lay there she heard a strange noise – a bit like a funny shouty bark.

Mia sat up. It sounded like it was coming from outside. She put her head under her curtains and peered out of the window. It was very dark, with only a bit of light coming from the lounge downstairs, where Mum and Dad were watching TV. As Mia's eyes got used to the darkness, she could make out more of the back garden. There was the shed, and the bird bath and her big brother Jamie's football, lying on the grass. Everything looked the same as it did in the daytime, just shadowy and strange somehow. She looked into the gardens of the houses next door.

On one side, Mr Cornish had his neat vegetable patch, with his plants all in rows. On the other side the garden couldn't be more different. There was a wilderness at the end of the garden, with trees and thick bushes. As Mia watched, something came out of the undergrowth and crept into the lawned area. At the same time, a cloud moved away from the moon and the gardens were bathed in moonlight. In the garden next door, there on the grass, were four baby foxes!

Mia watched in amazement as the four cubs played. She couldn't believe that this was happening just next door. She never would have known about it if she'd been asleep! The cubs chased each other around, pouncing and rolling in their play fights. A larger fox came and made the strange barking noise that Mia had heard earlier. As their mother called them, the cubs all raced into the bushes, out of sight.

Mia grinned to herself. It was magical!

She was about to get back into bed when another movement caught her eye. But this time it wasn't a fox. The old lady from next door got up from a bench in a shadowy corner of her garden. She'd been watching the fox cubs too!

The neighbour went inside without seeing Mia at her window. Mia ducked back under the curtains and sat on her bed, squeezing Tiger with happiness this time. It had been so amazing to see the cubs! It felt ... magic somehow.

I can't wait to tell Emily! Mia thought, before she remembered about their fight. She got a horrible uneasy feeling in her tummy again. She lay down and shut her eyes. She wouldn't think about Emily – not when she had something so nice to think about – excitable, gorgeous baby foxes!

❖

"And then the biggest cub jumped on the one with the fluffy tail," Mia told her dad excitedly over breakfast.

"It sounds like an amazing sight, you were lucky to see it!" Dad said.

Jamie came in wearing his football kit and grabbed some toast as Mia was talking. He was five years older than Mia, but they looked really similar – like a perfect mix of Mum and Dad. They both had dark hair and brown, almond-shaped eyes like Mum's. Mum was Chinese, but her family had lived in the UK ever since she was a baby. Dad was white with sandy-brown hair and blue eyes. Jamie was tall and broad like Dad, and Mia was silly and funny like him. Mia loved how she was a combinaion of both her parents.

She flicked her straight black hair over her shoulder as she told Jamie about the cubs.

"On TV?" he asked.

"No, in actual real life!" Mia told him. "And the lady next door saw them too!"

"Everyone at school says she's a witch." Jamie laughed.

"Jamie!" Dad said crossly. "That's not kind. She's just an old lady, that's all."

"No I'm not," Mum said, as she came into the kitchen, running a hand through her short black hair. "Although I feel like one some days."

"Not you!" Dad laughed. "The lady next

door. Mia saw her watching some fox cubs in her garden last night."

"Miss Philips? I think she works for a wildlife charity," Mum said. "She might know lots about foxes; you should ask her."

Mia remembered what Jamie had said and shook her head.

"Why don't you write her a letter and we'll pop it in to her later?" Dad suggested.

"OK!" Mia agreed. She'd love to know more about the fox cubs. Maybe they'd come again tonight!

After breakfast, Mia went back up to her room to write her letter. First she drew a picture of her favourite cub, the tiny one with the black socks on his feet. Then she wrote:

Dear Miss Philips.

My name is Mia and I live next door.

Last night I saw the foxes playing in your

*garden. I hope you don't mind but I saw
you watching them too. They are so cute.
My favourite is the little one. Have you
seen them before? Do you think they'll
come back tomorrow? Sorry to disturb
you,*

Love, Mia.

"Lovely," Dad said when she showed
it to him. "Are you going to take it round
now?"

Mia nodded. Dad gave her an envelope
for the letter and she licked the seal.
"There," she said. "Won't be long, Dad." She
walked quickly down their front path and
up to Miss Philips's house.

Mia knocked on the door. The old lady
approached to answer; Mia could see
her through the glass. When she opened
the door, Mia thought she did look a bit
like a witch. She had long, grey hair that

exploded around her shoulders messily, and her piercing blue eyes looked at Mia as if she could see all her secrets. But she was wearing a blue jumper with a picture of a happy hedgehog in the corner. Under the image, in curly writing, was APPLEDORE WILDLIFE SANCTUARY.

Mia gave her the letter.

Miss Philips looked at it in surprise, but when she opened it she smiled. Her eyes crinkled and suddenly she didn't look so scary any more.

"I call him Socks," she said, "the littlest cub."

Mia grinned. That was the perfect name! "What about the others?" she asked.

"I haven't named them yet," Miss Philips said. "Maybe you can help me think of some names for them?"

"Oh, yes! Do you think they'll come back tonight?" Mia said breathlessly.

Miss Philips nodded. "They'll be around. And as it gets lighter in the evenings we'll be able to see them more. Don't you have school holidays soon?"

"Easter holidays are next week!" said Mia.

"Perfect!" Miss Philips smiled. "That'll give us plenty of time for fox-spotting. Why don't you and your mum come and join me? You can get the best view from my garden, if you'd like to?"

Mia clasped her hands together in delight. "Yes please!"

🐾

"Thank you for having us, Miss Philips," Mia's mum said as Miss Philips ushered them inside later that evening. "Say thank you to Aunty Philips," she told Mia.

"Thank you!" Mia grinned.

"You're welcome," Miss Philips said.

"And call me Aunty Gwen, everyone else does." Her house was amazing. There were animals and plants everywhere. It was more like a zoo than a house.

As they passed the lounge Mia peeked in the open door and saw a fat tabby cat snoozing on a chair. On the rug in front of the fire was a black-and-white collie dog, who looked up and gave a quiet welcoming woof when he saw them.

Gwen led them into a big glass conservatory filled with plants. On a comfy-looking sofa was another cat, a white one this time. "You have so many pets!" Mia gasped.

Gwen waved her hand. "All rescues," she said. "They come to the wildlife sanctuary for help, and sometimes I can't resist bringing them home. I wish I could have more, there are so many animals who need a good home."

The dog padded up and pressed his nose

into her hand. Gwen ruffled his ears. "This is Duke. He's mainly deaf but he's a lovely old boy. The cats are Sally and Tabs."

Mia bent down to stroke Duke behind his ear. His tail wagged happily.

"I wish we could have a pet," Mia said, glancing at her mum, "but Mum and Dad always say no."

"The house is messy enough with just you and your brother," Mum told her firmly.

Gwen moved Sally the cat aside so they could sit down in the conservatory. Because it had glass walls they had a brilliant view of her garden. As soon as Mia sat down, Sally jumped up in her lap and curled up contentedly. She didn't mind that Mia was sitting in her spot – as long as she could still make herself comfortable! Mia giggled as she stroked the purring cat.

"It's lucky that you're on holiday this week," Gwen told her. "The cubs have been coming out of their hiding place for the past couple of weeks. Did you know that fox cubs are chocolatey brown when they first venture out of the den?"

Mia shook her head. "They didn't look brown," she said.

"No, these ones have got their smart red coats," Gwen told her. "I think they're about two months old."

Mia peered out of the large conservatory windows. At the bottom of the garden was a jungly bit full of overgrown bushes. "Is that where their den is?" she asked.

Gwen nodded. "But they've started exploring now. I've put a bit of dog food out for them, and they've been visiting me most days. You'll be able to see them playing every afternoon!"

"That sounds lovely, but Mia's going to be attending a drama class next week," Mum said.

Mia's heart sank. Emily and Zara would be there. She must have looked sad, because Mum and Gwen glanced at her with concerned faces. Gwen raised an eyebrow, her crinkly blue eyes full of curiosity.

"That sounds like fun, too," she said encouragingly.

Mia looked at Mum. "Do I have to go?" she asked.

Mum sighed. "Yes. Dad and I have to work, and Jamie will be at maths camp."

Mum turned to Gwen. "Usually my parents are around, but Lao Lao and Lao Ye are away on holiday at the moment." She turned back to Mia. "So you have to go to drama class. You were looking forward to it, remember?"

Mia looked at her feet. That was before Emily and Zara had made friends without her.

Gwen fixed her with a serious stare, but her blue eyes were twinkling.

"If you don't want to go to camp in your week off, maybe we can think of another solution. You can come and help out at the wildlife sanctuary with me in the mornings, and we could watch the cubs in the afternoon. I'm hoping my granddaughter will come and visit one day, and she's about your age. You'll be company for her."

Mia turned to Mum hopefully. Staying with Gwen would be brilliant – she wouldn't have to face Emily and Zara, and she could spend all her time with the fox cubs!

"I don't know, you were so looking forward to the camp..." Mum said.

"Please!" Mia pleaded.

"OK." Mum relented. "It's very kind of you. Why don't we try it tomorrow and see how it goes?"

Mia moved to hug Mum, forgetting Sally was on her lap. The cat jumped off with a cross meow.

"Oops!" Mia said. Gwen pretended to look very stern, but her smile gave it away.

"There's just one rule," she said. "Don't squash my cats!"

"I won't!" Mia laughed.

"What do you say to Gwen?" Mum asked.

"Thank you!" Mia flung her arms around her new friend. Suddenly the holidays seemed exciting after all!

♥ ❀ ★ ✿ 2 ✿ ★ ❀ ♥

"Now, remember to do whatever Aunty Philips says," Mum told Mia as she tied her long, dark hair into a long smooth ponytail.

"I will!" Mia said. She had got dressed carefully for her morning at the wildlife sanctuary, in black leggings and a T-shirt with a sparkly puppy on the front.

"And remember that these are wild animals, not pets," Mum continued. "They might bite. And don't go falling in love with any of them. You can't have a pet hedgehog, or a pet badger cub, or whichever one you think is cutest."

"Oh, but a pet badger would be so nice." Mia laughed. "I could call him Stripy!"

"No!" Mum finished Mia's hair and patted her on the bum with the hairbrush. "But most of all, be good. It's very kind of Aunty Gwen to look after you."

"I will," Mia promised. If today went well she could stay with Gwen the whole week, so she wasn't going to do anything to mess it up.

Gwen was wearing different, bottle-green jumper, but it had the same hedgehog logo and APPLEDORE WILDLIFE SANCTUARY written on it. She nodded at Mia's clothes approvingly.

"You just need one more thing," Gwen said.

She bent down and pinned a badge to Mia's T-shirt. VOLUNTEER it read in big letters, under a picture of the same hedgehog logo. Mia grinned happily.

"Ready?" Gwen asked.

"Yes!" Mia said in excitement.

"Have fun!" Mum said, "and thank you again!"

"No problem," Gwen replied. "I'm going to make her work hard!"

Mia felt a thrill. If the work involved animals, it was bound to be fun!

As Mum left for work, Gwen opened her car boot and Duke jumped in.

"Does Duke come to work with you every day?" Mia asked.

"Oh yes," Gwen replied. "I got him from the centre. He likes going back to see all his old friends."

Duke lay in his dog basket in the back, his tongue sticking out excitedly. Mia knew how he felt. She was so excited to be going to see all the animals that she felt like sticking her tongue out too!

"We look after a few cats or dogs that we

find homes for, but apart from them, all of the animals at the centre are wild," Gwen explained as she drove. "We want to release them back into the wild whenever we can, so we have to be really careful about touching them too much, we don't want to get them too used to humans."

Mia nodded. She'd been hoping that she could cuddle a fox cub, or stroke a squirrel, but not if it was bad for the animal. *It would be just as nice to see them up close*, she decided.

The sanctuary was a tiny little building at the edge of a park. Mia had been to the park loads of times with her family, but she'd never noticed the building, or the faded sign that read APPLEDORE WILDLIFE SANCTUARY.

Her heart whooshed with excitement as Gwen opened the door and called hello.

"Hello!" a woman's voice replied. They walked into a room that was filled with little pens all around the inside walls. In the middle of the room was a big table, and on it was a hedgehog!

Mia gasped. Gwen smiled. "We've got an extra helper for the next couple of weeks, Mandy," she told the lady.

"Brilliant!" Mandy glanced up and smiled at Mia. She had short brown hair and glasses, and her whole face was warm and friendly as she grinned. Mia liked her straight away.

"You can help me with Snuffles if you like," she said, carefully picking up the hedgehog. She had thick gloves on so that the prickles didn't hurt her hands. As she picked him up, the hedgehog tucked in his face and limbs so that he looked like a perfect ball of spikes. Mia knew that hedgehogs could curl up into a ball, but she'd never seen it happen before!

"Watch!" Mandy said. She carried the hedgehog to a nice clean pen, which had a dish full of dog food, and some crumpled paper bedding. She gently put him down, then she reached into a nearby pot and took out some tiny, crunchy-looking worms.

"These are dried mealworms, his favourite snack," Mandy said, putting a handful of them in front of Snuffles.

"Yuck!" Mia laughed.

For a minute, he stayed in a ball, but then, slowly, a pointy, snuffly little nose appeared, then two beady eyes and four cute little feet. The hedgehog snuffled around, sniffing the air and all around the pen, and gobbled up the mealworms, one by one. Then he padded over to the food and started munching it happily.

"He's so cute!" Mia whispered.

"We've got quite a few hedgehogs at the moment that were brought in because they were too small to hibernate," Mandy said.

"Hibernate?" Mia asked.

"That means they sleep all winter when it's cold, and wake up again when it's spring," Gwen explained. "Lots of animals hibernate – bears, squirrels and hedgehogs! But they need to get nice and fat so that they can sleep all winter without having to get up and find a snack."

"We've looked after them in the winter, and they'll be released soon now that it's spring. Snuffles is a bit different, though; he was brought in because he'd been bitten by a dog," Mandy said, showing Mia some neat stitches on his tummy. "But luckily his prickles kept him safe, and he's almost completely healed now. We'll be able to release him back where he was found soon, and he can go and tell his hedgehog friends all about his adventures!"

Mia grinned as the little hedgehog licked his lips and then shuffled into the pile of bedding for a nap.

"Right!" Gwen clapped her hands together. "We need to feed all the animals, make sure their enclosures are nice and clean, and give medicine to the animals that need it. Are you ready to help? I'm going to go outside to feed the bigger animals – can you help Mandy in here?"

Mia nodded. She glanced around at all the pens. She couldn't wait to see what was in each one!

Mandy left the hedgehog pen in its place next to the others and started wiping the table clean.

Mia peered around at all the pens, each of which was labelled with a tag. The hedgehog's label read: *Snuffles, bite wound, medicine twice daily*. In one pen was a family of mice all curled up asleep in a big ball. In another, an owl stood on a low perch and blinked at her sleepily.

Mandy put the next pen on the table.

"What do you think's inside?" she asked.

Mia looked at the label. FLOPSY, MOPSY AND COTTONTAIL, it read.

"Rabbits!" she guessed.

"Right! Well, we named them after rabbits, but actually these are baby hares. Do you know what they're called?" Mandy asked. Mia shook her head.

"Baby hares are called leverets," Mandy told her.

Mandy lifted out a load of straw, and there, snuggled together in a little straw circle that looked like a bird's nest, were three brown hares.

They blinked up curiously. They were very small and dusty brown, with bright black eyes and tiny stubby ears.

"They're so cute!" Mia squealed.

"Yes, they are lovely, aren't they?" Mandy said. "Someone found them in a field when they were only a couple of days old. Unlike rabbits, hares make little nests among the grass for their babies, rather than having them in burrows underground. Normally it's OK that they're alone because their mum leaves them during the day while she's eating, then comes back and feeds them when it gets dark, but the lady who brought these in watched them for two days and no one came."

Mia peered at the tiny bunnies, feeling sorry for them.

"We think the mum got eaten by a fox or something," Mandy explained.

A fox! Mia thought about Socks hunting a cute little bunny like this and shook her head to clear the image.

"It's the circle of life," Mandy said, realizing what Mia was thinking. "All animals have to eat, and not all of them like carrots. If the fox mum didn't go hunting, she wouldn't be able to bring food home for her cubs."

Mia nodded. She'd never thought about it like that before. Still, she was glad these hares were safe – they were so cute!

"We've fed these little ones and they're nearly ready to be released into the wild." Mandy put her hand in and the bunnies hopped around the box, moving surprisingly quickly. But Mandy was quicker. She grabbed one and held it up.

"We have to try not to handle them much. It makes it harder for them to survive in the wild if they lose their fear of people."

"What can I do?" Mia asked.

"We just need to clean out this pen for them," Mandy said. "So pass me that box..."

Mia rushed to grab a box from the side and Mandy carefully put the wriggling bunny on the table, turning it upside down and checking it all over. "Yep, looks nice and healthy," she said.

The bunny looked perfect to Mia! It had surprisingly big feet, and it kept kicking them as if it was trying to hop out of Mandy's hands.

Mandy popped it in the box and it hopped, shaking its fur crossly. Its fluffy white tail looked as soft as a cloud and Mia longed to touch it!

"Do you want to get the next one?" Mandy asked.

"Me?" Mia was so surprised that her voice came out in a squeak.

"Yes!" Mandy replied. "Just reach in and grab one, gently but firmly. Like this!" Mandy put her hand in the pen. The two remaining hares hopped out of the way, but she caught one firmly around her middle. She squirmed, kicking her feet out, but Mandy stroked her forehead. "Shh, shh," she said. Then she checked her ears, feet and bum, and put her in the box with her sister.

"Your turn!" she said with a grin. Mia felt her heart beating fast. She really wanted to hold the little hare, but she didn't want to scare it, or drop it.

"Put both hands in and grab her around the middle," Mandy instructed. "But nice and gently. You'll have to get used to moving animals if you're going to help out here!"

Mia rolled up her sleeves and put her arms in the pen. The last leveret was in a corner, looking up at her as if it was terrified.

"I'm not going to hurt you," Mia murmured. "I just need to pick you—" as she spoke she put her arms down towards the hare. It jumped, and Mia caught it, mid-hop. "Up!" she finished, in delight. It was so cuddly and warm, and Mia could feel its heart beating fast through its soft fur.

"You're a natural!" Mandy said, and Mia

felt a rush of pride. "Hold her still while I check her."

Mia let her thumb stroke over the hare's back as Mandy did the checks. "She's fine too!" Mandy said. "Great stuff. Put her in with the others."

Mia carefully held the rabbit over the box. Her back legs started wriggling as she saw her sisters and she kicked out, impatient to be free.

"It's OK, let her go," Mandy said as Mia struggled to hold on to her. Mia dropped the baby hare into the box and she hopped over to her sisters. Soon they were huddled together so tight that Mia couldn't tell which one she'd picked up.

"That was amazing!" She grinned at Mandy.

"You did brilliantly," Mandy said. "Now for the less fun part." She got out fresh newspaper and straw and showed Mia how to clean out the pen, and replace the food with some new pellets and some fresh grass and dandelions.

Mia helped Mandy clean out the pen, looking curiously at the straw nest the bunnies had been cuddled up in. "It looks like it's for birds," she said shyly.

Mandy grinned. "Yes, it's funny, isn't it? I didn't know hares built little nests until I started working here. It's called a 'form', and they make it in long grass so predators can't see the babies. Because of the nests, people used to think that hares hatched out of eggs, and that's why we have the Easter bunny giving out Easter eggs!"

While Mandy laid fresh newspaper at the bottom of the pen, Mia carefully molded the straw into a nice new nest. "Perfect!" Mandy said.

Mia put the nest in the pen, then Mandy carefully transferred all three bunnies back in. They hopped over to the nest and jumped straight in, huddling together so closely that Mia could only tell there were three of them by counting their fluffy tails.

"What now?" Mia said eagerly as they put the pen away. She couldn't wait to see what animal she'd meet next!

The morning passed so quickly as Mandy and Mia cleaned out each cage one by one. Gwen and Duke came back inside, shaking the rain off their coats. "Look at the time!" she cried.

There was a grumbly growl. "Was that you?" Mia asked Duke, who had flopped under the table. He lifted his head off his paws and looked at her innocently.

Gwen laughed "Don't blame Duke – that was my tummy! I think it's lunchtime."

"Oh!" Mia complained. She didn't want to go home, she was having so much fun.

"I'm glad you're enjoying yourself!" Gwen said, "But we'll be back tomorrow. And didn't you have some little foxes you were excited about seeing this afternoon?" Gwen raised an eyebrow.

Mia gasped – she'd almost forgotten about Socks! "I do want to see the foxes playing," she said, "as long as we can come back tomorrow."

"What do you think, Mandy?" Gwen teased. "Can Mia come back?"

Mia turned to Mandy. She knew they were only teasing but the answer still mattered.

"We'd be lucky to have her help," Mandy said kindly.

Mia felt a warm buzz of pride. It had only been one morning, but she felt like she wanted to work at the sanctuary for ever!

3

Mia held her breath as the foxes emerged. She and Gwen were sitting silently in the conservatory. Duke was lying next to Mia with his heavy head on her lap. He looked up curiously when he spotted the movement in the garden, but she stroked his ears and he lay back down again.

It was late afternoon. They'd had a lunch of thick cheese-and-pickle sandwiches and taken Duke for a walk. Then they'd scattered some puppy food on the grass for the foxes to eat, and settled down in the conservatory to wait. Mia had been disappointed when the foxes hadn't appeared straight away.

She'd sat with her eyes fixed on the messy grass at the bottom of the garden, watching for the slightest movement. But there had been nothing. Soon Mum would be home from work and come and pick her up.

Gwen had fallen asleep in the chair next to her, but when the clock bonged three o'clock she woke up with a start.

"Three o'clock, you know what that means?" she said.

Mia shook her head.

"Ice cream time!" Gwen said. "My granddaughter always has three o'clock ice cream when she comes to visit. Would you like some?"

"Yes please!" Mia said.

Gwen fetched them each a bowl, and got the animals a treat too.

"Thank you," Mia said as Gwen handed her the bowl. But as she turned to Gwen, something outside caught her eye.

"Look!" Gwen said, noticing it too.

Mia gasped as she saw something moving at the end of the garden. The bushes shook, and then, carefully, cautiously, the mother fox stepped out.

She roamed around the garden cautiously. She went right up to the food Gwen had put out for them. Then she gave a yipping, barking noise, and the babies appeared.

"One, two, three!" Mia counted delightedly as one after another the three cubs came tumbling out of the undergrowth. They scampered around and jumped over each other excitedly, as they raced over to their mum.

But when Socks came out of the bushes, Gwen sat forward. He was limping. As he hobbled over to the food Mia could see that he was holding one of his front legs up in the air as he moved. It must be hurt!

"Oh, no!" she gasped. "Poor Socks."

"Yes, that doesn't look very good at all," Gwen said.

"Will it get better?" Mia asked.

"Let's keep an eye on him for a couple of days. If it's just a sprain, it might heal on its own," Gwen told her. "What shall we call his brothers and sisters?"

Mia examined them all. The biggest one ran straight over to the food and started chomping it down. "We could call him Greedy," she laughed. "But that's not a very nice name. How about Rusty?"

Gwen laughed too. "That's a good name. I think that one's a girl," she said, pointing at the one with the fluffy tail. "Her coat looks so soft and velvety. How about Velvet?"

"Yes!" Mia agreed. "And the last one is Pouncer!"

Gwen laughed as the third cub jumped on Rusty's tail. "Rusty, Velvet, Pouncer and

Socks," she said. "Those are all excellent names."

While the other three played, Socks was standing still. The mum fox went over to Socks and nudged him towards the food with her nose, but Socks just whimpered sadly and sat down in one of Gwen's overgrown flower beds.

They watched the cubs' rough and tumble, exploring the garden, but Mia couldn't take her eyes off Socks. "I think the mum fox is worried, too," she whispered. The vixen stood watch over them all, her ears twitching, then she collected some food and dropped it near Socks. He barely moved and he kept giving a high-pitched whine. When his brothers and sister came over, he let them eat the food, just watching them tussling for the best bits and pouncing on each other.

Mia's heart twisted as she watched the

poor little cub. "Can we do anything?" she asked Gwen quietly.

Gwen had just opened her mouth to reply when a noise startled the foxes. The mother fox turned towards the fence and looked at it, her ears twitching anxiously. Then she barked a warning, and in seconds all the cubs disappeared into the long grass. Socks limped after them.

"I wonder what spooked them?" Gwen said. Then a football sailed over the fence.

"Jamie!" Mia said crossly. Gwen opened the back door and Mia went out to get the ball.

"You scared my foxes!" she shouted at her brother. Jamie didn't reply. Mia bashed the fence loudly enough for her brother to hear even with his earphones in.

"Hello?" he called.

"Your stupid ball scared my foxes!" Mia yelled.

"Mia?" Jamie sounded confused. "What are you doing next door?"

Mia huffed in irritation. Now the foxes were gone and she wouldn't get to see if Socks ate anything. He didn't look very well at all. She stomped back to Gwen's house.

"Do you think he'll be OK?" Mia asked.

"We'll keep an eye on him, and so will his mum," Gwen promised. "Don't worry."

But Mia couldn't help feeling concerned. She looked out into the garden and crossed her fingers tightly. *Please be OK, Socks.*

"I'm glad that you had a good day," Mum said as they sat eating dinner that night.

"And it seems like you're learning lots about animals too," Dad agreed.

"I'd learn even more about animals if I could have one of my own..." Mia suggested hopefully.

"Not going to happen!" Mum replied, like she always did. "Oh, I forgot to say, Emily phoned for you!"

Mia felt her heart jump. She'd had such a good day that she hadn't been thinking about her best friend at all ... if she *was* still her best friend.

"What did she say?" she asked.

"She asked whether you wanted to go round to her house tomorrow," Mum said. "Her mum said she didn't enjoy camp today, so she's not going back. I said yes, I hope that's OK?"

Mia chewed on her lip. If Emily wasn't having fun at camp maybe that's because she was missing her – maybe she and Zara weren't friends any more!

She grinned. "Thanks, Mum!" But then she remembered the plans she'd made, all the animals at the sanctuary. She didn't want to let them down. "Can I go just in the afternoon? I said I would go back to the wildlife centre tomorrow morning."

"OK," Mum said. "I'll call Emily's mum and see if she will come and get you after lunch tomorrow."

Mia grinned. Perfect! The morning with the animals and the afternoon with Emily. She couldn't wait to tell her all about Socks! She peered out into the garden. She hoped he was OK, curled up safely in his den with his brothers and sister.

4

"Come here, quietly. I've got a surprise for you," Gwen whispered as she opened the front door.

"Why are we whispering?" Mia whispered back.

But Gwen just put her fingers to her lips.

Mia had no idea what was going on, but she tiptoed inside as quietly as she could.

Gwen led her into the lounge. "Stay, Duke," she said, to Mia's surprise. Duke plonked himself down on his bum obediently, but he gave a soft whine as Gwen walked away.

Mia stroked the old dog's head as he looked up at her curiously.

Gwen opened the conservatory door and beckoned Mia inside, putting her finger to her lips again. Then she shut the door carefully behind them.

In a corner of the conservatory was a big pen, the same kind as they had in the wildlife sanctuary. It had a wooden frame and wire mesh covering the sides. And inside, curled up on a cosy bed of straw, with his tail wrapped around his legs just the way she'd imagined last night, was Socks!

Mia held her breath as she walked slowly towards him. It was amazing to see him so close! His nose was long and pointed, and he had fine black whiskers and a black nose a bit like Duke's.

Even though they were being as quiet as possible, the fox cub's ears twitched and he raised his head, blinking at them sleepily. He gave a huge yawn, showing his pointy teeth and pink tongue. Then he shifted his tail and Mia caught sight of a thick, bright-pink plaster cast on his poorly front leg. Even his paw was completely hidden by it. The cast stuck out in front of him and he rested his chin on it sadly.

"What happened?" Mia whispered.

"After you'd gone last night, I realized he was still in the garden," Gwen explained. "I went to put food and water near him. Normally that's what the animal sanctuary tell people to do, and keep an eye on them for a day. But when I got closer I could see his leg was broken. I called the vet from the wildlife centre and she came and had a look at him. He'll need medicine every few hours, so we decided he can stay here until his leg's better." Gwen smiled. "I could do with some help."

"Yes please!" Mia said. She couldn't take her eyes off the adorable fox cub. She was very sorry that his leg was hurt, but she loved the thought of spending more time with him.

"Remember, he's a wild animal," Gwen said. "If he gets too used to people, it could cause him problems when he's older. We have to treat him like a wild creature, not a pet."

"I will," Mia promised.

She knelt next to the pen. His black eyes watched her intently as she moved, but he didn't seem frightened. Up close she could see his fur wasn't just red, it was brown and gold too, with white fur under his chin and on his chest, and as well as the black socks on his feet, he had black tips on his ears. He was so gorgeous.

Duke whined and scratched at the conservatory door, wondering why he wasn't allowed in, and Socks shifted at the sound. Then he lifted his back leg and scratched his ear, as if he was a dog with fleas. Mia couldn't help giggling.

"He's lovely, isn't he?" Gwen said. "Do you want to feed him?"

"Can I?" Mia gasped.

Gwen nodded. "I've got some milk with his medicine in; do you want to give it to him?"

"Yes, please!" Mia said.

Gwen went to the kitchen and came back with a big plastic syringe full of milk.

She pulled on some thick gardening gloves, and opened the pen. Socks put his front paws on the open door and peered out at them.

"Hi!" Mia whispered.

Gwen carefully picked Socks up by the skin at the back of his neck. He made a little growling noise. "This is how his mum carries him and his brothers and sister around. It doesn't hurt them," Gwen said.

Socks's legs wriggled in the air and he gave a yip.

"Good boy," Gwen soothed him. She put a tea towel on her lap and held him there with one gloved hand.

"Now, put the syringe up to his mouth like this." She took the syringe and showed Mia how to quickly squeeze some milk into the cub's mouth. He drank it, and then licked his lips happily.

"Now you try!" Gwen said, passing the syringe over to Mia.

Mia put it close to his mouth. "*Yip yip!*" Socks said, wriggling on Gwen's lap.

"Open up!" Mia said. She put the tip of the plastic tube on his lip and squeezed it gently. Socks turned his head and the milk dribbled down his chin.

"Oops!" Mia said. But Socks's pink

tongue came out and licked it all up. "He likes it!" Mia said.

"Try again," Gwen said encouragingly.

Mia gave Socks the tip of the syringe again. This time it all went in, and Socks licked his nose clean. Then he gave a happy chattering noise as if he was saying, "More please!"

"OK, greedy guts." Mia laughed. "You're even hungrier than your brother, Rusty!"

She fed him the whole syringe, a little bit at a time. When it was all gone, Socks chattered for more.

"It's all gone!" she told him.

"He can have some other food as well," Gwen told her. "I've got some puppy food for him, and we can give him some minced meat: that's what we'd give him at the centre. By the time his leg's better, he'll be the biggest one of the litter, not the smallest!"

Socks was full of energy, scrabbling at

Gwen's gloves and trying to wriggle off her lap.

He looked so soft and fluffy, and Mia longed to touch him.

"Go on, I know you want to!" Gwen said.

"What?" Mia asked.

"You can give him a tiny stroke, a little one won't hurt," Gwen told her. Mia reached out and touched the top of his head. His fur was as soft and fine as dandelion fluff, and he was warm and wriggly.

He flipped over as if he wanted her to stroke his belly. "He's so friendly! I don't think he'd bite!" Mia said.

"We don't have to stay away from him to protect *us*," Gwen explained. "It's for his sake. We want him to go back into the wild and be safe, and for that he needs to stay away from people."

Mia nodded. She gave him one last pet then pulled her hands away. When she had seen the foxes from her window that night she never thought she'd get this near to them. It was enough of a treat to see him close up and look after him.

Gwen put Socks back into his pen, and filled up his food bowl with the puppy food. Socks stood stiffly, his injured leg sticking out at an angle, and hopped over to the meat. He gulped it down and then looked up at them, licking his lips.

Mia watched at the happy cub and felt her heart swell with love.

"We're going to look after you, Socks," she said. "I promise."

5

"Mia!" Emily shrieked as she came running down the driveway of her house. She was wearing a glittery yellow T-shirt and her short, curly blonde hair bobbed up and down as she ran. Mia and Gwen had spent the morning with Socks, and then Emily's mum had come to pick her up. Mia couldn't wait to tell Emily about her fox cub!

Mia got out of the car and Emily gave her a big hug. Mia felt a thrill of happiness. "I've missed you!" Emily said.

"Me too!" said Mia.

"I've got so much to tell you! Camp was so rubbish," Emily said as they started walking inside. "I only spend one day there and it was the worst day of my entire life!"

"What happened?" Mia asked, giggling at her friend's dramatic face.

"The teacher was so bossy!" Emily said. "It was like being in the army!"

She opened the kitchen door, and there, at the table, was Zara. She had on a glittery top that matched Emily's, and the table was covered in glitter and crafty bits.

"Hi, Mia!" Zara said. "Are you talking about Ms Diaz?" Zara stood up and pretended to be wearing glasses. "I told you girls to sit down!" she said in a funny voice. She and Emily burst into laughter.

"Zara brought her glitter designer," Emily told Mia. "You can draw designs with the pens, and then put it in this little machine and it makes anything glittery! Isn't it cool?"

"Sorry, there were only two T-shirts,"

Zara said, glancing up at Mia. "But you can do a badge?"

"No, thanks," Mia said, even though they did look really nice. Her throat was hurting as she tried not to cry. Emily hadn't said Zara would be there. And now they had matching T-shirts and she was left out again.

It was the same all afternoon. Zara and Emily kept talking and laughing about their time at camp, and Emily did whatever Zara wanted. Emily's mum offered them pizza or sandwiches for tea, and Emily chose sandwiches like Zara, even though Mia knew pizza was her favourite. Or at least it used to be. Just like Mia used to be her favourite friend.

Mia wished she was back with Gwen and Socks. She hadn't even had chance to tell Emily about the fox cub. Emily and Zara had spent the whole afternoon pretending to be bossy Ms Diaz.

"Girls, I've got a surprise for you – Easter egg hunt!" Emily's mum called.

"Easter eggs! Yum!" Zara jumped up and ran into the other room. Emily followed her. Rolling her eyes, Mia followed them too. Emily's mum was standing by the back door, holding Emily's baby sister, who was already happily eating some chocolate.

"There are fifteen small chocolate eggs hidden in the garden," Emily's mum said, "five each. Emily, yours are blue, Zara, yours are pink, and Mia, yours are gold. And there's one extra big super egg for the person who finds it – but it's hidden in a VERY difficult place. Look high, look low ... and be careful of my rose bush!"

"Come on!" Emily grabbed Mia's hand. She giggled and tried not to mind that Emily grabbed Zara with her other hand. Together, they raced out into the garden.

Mia's eyes darted around, looking for any trace of gold.

"Got one!" Zara called out.

Mia looked even harder. She wouldn't let Zara find hers first! She saw a flash of gold resting in a plant pot and ran over to pick it up.

Emily was over by her Wendy house, looking around it. Mia laughed as she spotted a blue egg on the low roof of the house. It was right above Emily's head! "Emily!" she called, and pointed up.

Emily saw the egg and grabbed it, laughing.

Mia kept hunting. She found another shining gold egg on the windowsill of the Wendy house, and one hiding at the bottom of the washing-line pole. She found a pink one resting on the watering can but left it for Zara to find, and she saw another of Emily's blue ones on the garden swing. Then she spotted a gold glimmer in the grass and raced towards it. Her last one was balanced on top of the bird table. She had her five eggs, but there was still the mysterious big egg to find. Mia looked around the garden. Zara was hunting around the flower bed, and as Mia watched she reached out and grabbed a pink egg. "Got all my small eggs!" she called.

"So have I," Mia told her.

"I've only got two!" Emily squealed. She ran across the garden, straight past the blue egg that was resting on the swing. Mia grinned at her friend. Emily was still hunting for her little eggs, so it was between her and Zara. Who would find the big egg first?

Mia was determined to win! She scoured the garden, looking as hard as she did when he was trying to spot the foxes at the very bottom of Gwen's garden.

She looked all around the Wendy house, and in all the flower beds. *Where could it be?*

"I've looked everywhere!" Zara squealed.

Mia looked around again. Emily's mum was standing next to her rose bush. And hidden in it was something colourful ... Emily's mum hadn't been telling them *not* to go near the rose bush – she'd been giving them a clue!

Mia raced towards the rose bush as fast as she could. Out of the corner of her eye she spotted Zara heading over to it too. She was getting closer and closer. Mia ran faster, pretending that she had powerful legs like the baby hares. She'd just got close to it when ... *oof!* Something hit her foot and she fell in a heap on the grass.

Zara raced up to the bush and grabbed the egg from underneath it. "I got it!" she crowed.

"You tripped me!" Mia yelled.

"No, I didn't!" Zara said, looking surprised.

"You did! You knew I was going to win so you tripped me up," Mia shouted.

Emily came over and looked from one girl to the other.

"If Zara says she didn't..." she said with a shrug.

Mia felt like crying. Of course Emily would take Zara's side.

Emily's mum came over, holding the baby. "Hey, what's all this?" she asked. "There's no need to fight, I've got big eggs for the runners-up too," she told them.

"I would have got it but Zara tripped me up," Mia exclaimed. "She's a cheat."

"Am NOT," Zara said, looking like she was going to cry.

"OK, OK, OK, " Emily's mum soothed. "Well done, everyone. Now let's go inside and you can eat your chocolate and watch a film, all right?"

Mia shot Zara a horrid look. Zara grabbed Emily's hand and they went inside.

Mia followed them miserably, feeling worse than ever before.

🐾

When Emily's mum dropped her off later, Mia glanced at Gwen's house sadly. She wondered how Socks was doing, and if his brothers and sister had played in the garden that afternoon.

"Can I go and visit?" she asked Mum. "Gwen said I can help feed him."

"Go on then," Mum said. "If it's OK with Gwen. But be back in time for tea at five o'clock. You need feeding too!"

Mia knocked on the door and grinned as Duke barked.

"Mia!" Gwen said happily. "I didn't

think we were seeing you this afternoon!"

"I came back early," Mia explained. "How's Socks?"

"He's OK," Gwen said. "He's been a bit miserable, I don't know why. He's been taking his medicine so his leg shouldn't be too sore..."

They went into the conservatory. Socks started yipping as he saw them. He paced up and down in the pen and looked at them, his black eyes sad.

"I've just fed him," Gwen said, "so he should be full of beans..."

Socks looked as sad as she felt, Mia thought. Perhaps he was feeling lonely, just like she was.

"Maybe he misses his family?" Mia said. "I know!" She jumped up so fast that she startled Socks and he jumped too.

"Sorry, Socks!" She giggled. "I'm just going to get something from my house,

OK?" Gwen looked confused, but she nodded.

Mia ran out of Gwen's house and up her own garden path. She hammered on the door. Mum answered it, talking in Cantonese on the phone. Mia could only understand a few words, but she knew Mum must be talking to her grandparents. "Say hi from me!" she said as she hurried inside.

"Back already?" Mum asked.

"I just need to get something!" Mia said, rushing past. She ran up the stairs, two at a time, and burst into her bedroom. Then she flung open her wardrobe and started looking though all the toys at the bottom. *It was in here somewhere ...* Toys flew all over her bedroom floor as she pulled them out of the cupboard.

"What are you doing?" Mum asked from the doorway. She'd finished on the phone and was standing with her hands on her hips. "You'd better clear that up, young lady."

"I will! I just need something for Socks – aha!" Mia grinned as she found what she was looking for – a toy fox! Her grandparents, Lao Lao and Lao Ye, had bought him for her a few years ago, but she'd never played with him much.

"I think Socks is lonely," she explained. "We can't touch him much because it's bad for him, but he can cuddle up to this!"

"What a good idea!" Mum said. "Oh, and I know something else that might help." She led Mia downstairs. In the kitchen she put the kettle on and hunted in the cupboard under the sink. She brought out a hot-water bottle with a fluffy cover.

"Oh!" Mia said happily. "It'll be warm and furry, just like cuddling up with his brothers and sister!"

"Exactly!" Mum gave Mia a high five. She filled up the hot-water bottle and screwed the lid in tightly.

"Thanks, Mum!" Mia grabbed the hot-water bottle, blew her mum a kiss, and taking her gifts, rushed back next door.

Gwen gave a huge smile as she saw what Mia had brought. "Why didn't I think of that? We often give soft toys to animals at the centre."

"Do you think he'll like it?" Mia asked.

"Let's go and find out!" Gwen replied.

They went back into the conservatory. Socks jumped up when they came in, padding over to the bars.

Gwen opened the metal door of the pen and put the toy and the hot-water bottle in a cosy spot right at the back.

"Yip yip yip!" Socks gave his funny bark as the new things appeared in his pen. But then he came over, looking curious. He gave them such a big sniff that he knocked the toy fox over. Then he clamoured over it, barking as if he wanted it to play.

"His tail's wagging like a dog's!" Mia said with a giggle.

Finally he settled down next to the hot-water bottle, his mouth hanging open in a foxy grin.

"I think he likes them!"

Gwen put her arm around Mia's shoulders as Socks played. "You know, if your mum ever lets you, I think you'd be a very good pet owner," she said. "It was so clever of you to realize how he must be feeling."

Mia felt a thrill of pride.

Socks played happily, then curled up in a ball next to the hot-water bottle, his nose tucked into his tail.

He looked so cute! Mia took a picture on her phone to show her mum.

"I think this calls for a special late ice

cream time," Gwen said, a twinkle in her eye. "Don't you agree?"

"Oh yes!" Mia said with a grin. She'd cheered Socks up – and he'd cheered her up too!

6

"Mia, come and see!" Mandy called as they arrived at the wildlife sanctuary the next day. Her voice was high and excited. Mia and Gwen had just got to the centre with Duke. Gwen shrugged and Mia put down her bag and raced inside.

Mandy was peering into a pen that was usually empty. "We've got a new arrival," she said happily, "look!"

In a pen was a little orange cat. He had stripy ginger fur and a white patch on his tummy. He backed away into a corner, but as he did so, Mandy grinned at Mia and said, "Look at his feet!"

"He's got socks too!" Mia noticed with a smile. He had white socks on his front paws, just like Socks's black ones!

Mia reached out to stroke the adorable cat, but he flinched away and cowered at the back of the pen. "He's so scared," Mia said.

"He was a stray," Mandy explained. "He doesn't seem to like people much."

Just then the cat gave a sneeze, and then another and another. "He's got cat flu," Mandy told Mia. "He'll need lots of looking after, and when he's completely better we'll hopefully find him a home of his own."

Mia looked at the little cat. He looked as wild as Socks, but instead of that being a good thing, it was a bit sad. She hoped he'd find a lovely family.

"What shall we call him?" Mandy said.

"Well, we can't call him Socks!" Mia said. "We'll get too confused!"

"We'll think of something." Mandy said. "Now come on, we've got lots of animals to look after."

Flopsy, Mopsy and Cottontail the hares had been released back into the wild, and Mia missed them, but there were plenty more animals that needed help.

Mandy had taken one of the hedgehogs out, and Mia was leaving a trail of his favourite snack – crunchy dried mealworms – for him to follow. It was so cute to watch him. He snuffled up to each one, sniffing the table, chewed it nosily with his mouth open, then snuffled up to the next one.

"Careful!" Mia laughed as he snuffled close to the edge of the table.

Just then the phone rang. "Appledore Wildlife Sanctuary," Gwen answered. "A swan!" she exclaimed.

Mia and Mandy both turned to look at

her. "Swan, damaged wing," Gwen said. Mandy nodded and started moving more things off the table. "We'll have to make room," she said.

Mandy carefully picked up the Snuffles the hedgehog and popped him in with another hedgehog. "He'll be all right in there for a minute," she told Mia.

"I think you might have to sit this one out, Mia," Gwen said. "Swans can be dangerous. They have a very strong beak and wings – a swan's wing has been known to break people's arms. If it's in pain it might lash out – animals don't mean to hurt us, but they don't understand that we're trying to help them."

"How about helping out with the cat while we're busy?" Mandy suggested.

"Good idea!" Gwen said.

Mia nodded. "I'll do anything to help, even if it means cleaning out lots of poo!"

Gwen laughed. "Thank you for that, and I'll bear it in mind, but this is a clean job!"

She took Mia into the staffroom, which had lots of lockers, a table and chairs, and an old, saggy green sofa.

"Sit there a minute," Gwen said. Mia sat down, wondering what was going to happen next.

Gwen reappeared with something wriggling in her arms – the ginger cat! She carefully shut the door behind her, then put it down. The cat shot out of her arms and ran straight under the table.

"He needs a bit of rehabilitation," Gwen explained. "Unlike all the wild animals, we need to get him used to human beings. No one will adopt him unless he gets a bit friendlier."

"Gwen!" Mandy called from the other room.

"Could you sit with him a minute." Gwen asked. "I don't expect he'll go anywhere near you, but just talk to him, and stroke him if you can. It's the opposite of dealing with Socks – touch him as much as possible!"

"Yes, fine, don't worry," Mia said. Gwen was already halfway out of the door. Mia thought about the poor swan and hoped it would be OK.

As Gwen carefully shut the door, Mia got off the sofa and peered under the table. Two big eyes stared back at her. The cat was right at the back, the way he had been in the pen.

The room was quiet, it was just her and the cat. *What had Gwen said?* Mia thought. *Talk to it.* "I'm Mia," she said. She bent down and looked under the table, but her hair got in her face. So she lay down so that she could see the cat and he could see her. *What am I going to talk about?*

"Hi," she said. The cat didn't move. "You don't have to be scared of me. I won't hurt you. I know you're scared and you don't like people." She thought about Zara tripping her up and lying about it. "Sometimes I don't think people are very nice, either."

She peeked at the kitten. He didn't move, but his ears were pointed at her. Mia decided that meant that he was listening to her. "But I'm nice," she told him, "and so are lots of other people. And we're going to find some lovely people to adopt you, and then you'll have food every day and a nice warm house to sleep in."

It was funny, Socks didn't have those things, but it didn't feel the same when she thought about him being outside. He was *meant* to be in the wild, running around with his brothers and sister, hunting in the moonlight. But when Mia thought about this cat being outside, all alone, it hurt her heart. Cats were meant to be stroked and loved. This one was very thin. Mia wished she could tell him not to be frightened.

She shuffled closer to the cat on her belly, her top half under the table and her legs sticking out. As she got closer, Mia put her hand out and let him sniff it. He leaned forward to sniff and Mia had to hide her happiness. "Good boy," she soothed softly. "See, we can be friends." She put her hand up to the top of his head and stroked his ears. His fur was so soft, and he nudged his head into her hand impatiently, asking for more. "You're such a lovely boy," Mia said. "You aren't a wild thing, are you? You're a lost thing. You need a lovely home and a family of your very own."

The cat flopped over on to his back, all four white socks in the air, and rolled about delightedly as Mia stroked his head. Mia giggled. "It would be easier to do this if we weren't under a table," she said with a laugh.

The cat flipped over and looked at her seriously. "Meow," he said.

"What shall we call you?" Mia said. "I've already got a Socks, but your little white paws are so cute ... how about Boots?"

"Meow!" the cat said.

"I think that means you like it!" Mia said. "Good boy, Boots! Let's see what Gwen gave us to play with." She backed out from under the table and went to the pen. There were a few cat toys, a mouse and a fish on a piece of elastic.

Mia dangled the fish at the edge of the table, trying to tempt him out. She flopped the fish along the floor, and to her delight a tiny white cat paw came out and batted at it. But when she tried to move it away from the table, to get Boots to come out, he didn't budge.

"You're too clever, aren't you?" Mia said, peering under the table again.

As soon as he saw her, Boots turned over for another stroke. Mia laughed. "OK, I'll come to you. But you can't stay under the table for ever."

She crawled back under the table and stroked Boots there. "If only making friends with people was this easy," she sighed. Boots looked up at her as if he understood every word.

"We're friends, aren't we?" Mia said.

Boots gave a deep purr.

Mia was so busy stroking him that she didn't even hear the door open.

"Mia!" Gwen laughed out loud as she saw Mia's legs poking out from under the table. "What are you doing under there?" Gwen bent down to look under the table. She took one glance at Mia stroking Boots and her mouth dropped open.

"We're making friends!" Mia told her.

"I still can't believe it," Gwen as they pulled into her driveway. "You did such a good job with Boots. No one in the centre has been able to go anywhere near him at all."

Mia felt a flutter of pride. It had been a fun morning. She and Boots had played while everyone else looked after the swan. It had had a piece of plastic stuck around its wing, but it had been in so much pain that it had fought all the rescue staff that were trying to help it. The vet had given it an injection to put it to sleep while they untangled it. They'd managed to get all the plastic off, and given the swan some antibiotics. It would have to stay in the hospital overnight, but it would be released back into the wild tomorrow. When Gwen and Mia had left, it was looking much happier and tucking into a meal of fresh greens and wildfowl pellets.

Mia and Gwen had stayed late at the centre to help finish all the normal chores. Mia didn't mind being late home, she only had two days left of the Easter holidays and she wanted to spend as much time as she could at the centre.

"When do you think Socks can go back to the wild?" Mia asked.

"It normally takes about six weeks for a fracture to heal," Gwen told her, "so I'll have him for about four weeks longer."

Mia felt a mix of happy and sad. She wanted Socks to be well, but she loved seeing him every day.

Suddenly she had a horrible thought – next week she'd be back at school! How would she see Socks and all the other animals then? "Can I keep helping out even when I go back to school?" she asked.

"Do you want to?" Gwen asked her. "Won't you have lots of other, more fun, things to do, rather than cleaning up after animals?"

"Oh, but I love it!" Mia said. "Meeting the animals, helping look after them – it was so much fun!"

"You certainly seem to have a way with animals." Gwen smiled. "I'll have to talk to your parents, but I don't see why you can't keep helping at the centre at the weekends. And you can come round and see Socks every day after school while he's still with me."

Mia grinned in delight. Five more weeks of Socks!

Mia woke up the next morning still with a smile on her face. Sunshine was streaming into her yellow bedroom, and she could smell breakfast cooking downstairs. It was Sunday, so she wasn't going to the centre, but Gwen said she could go round and see Socks later.

When she got to Gwen's, the house was a flurry of activity. It was tidier than usual, and Gwen had her wild hair pinned up in a neat clip that looked like a shell.

"My granddaughter is coming around today as well!" Gwen said happily. "She's about your age, so hopefully you'll get on. Her family have just moved to a house not too far away, so I'm hoping I'll get to see her much more. Her mum doesn't like animals," she confided in a whisper, "but my granddaughter does!"

Mia had never seen Gwen look so happy. "I'm sure she'll love to meet Socks," she said. She imagined Gwen's granddaughter would be a young version of Gwen, with messy hair and animal fur on all her clothes. Even if she didn't like animals as much as Gwen, she'd love to see Socks – who wouldn't?

"I've just got to finish my baking – I'm making banana bread, it's my grandaughter's favourite," Gwen said. "Do you want to give Socks his lunch?"

Socks was laid with his chin on his cast again, looking out of the glass conservatory door. "Do you think he misses his family?" Mia said.

"He'll be back with them soon," Gwen told her. "His leg seems a bit better already. Watch this." She held out a piece of chicken and gave a low whistle. Socks sniffed the air and turned. When he saw the treat he struggled to his feet and walked, stiff-legged, over to the edge of the pen.

Gwen dropped the chicken and he gobbled it up eagerly. Then he looked up at them, licking his lips.

While Gwen disappeared into the kitchen, Mia fed more scraps of meat through the bars of the pen, and Socks raced to get them. When it was all gone, Socks sat down and started to lick his paws like a happy cat.

Mia giggled. He did seem better.

The doorbell rang and Gwen squealed in the kitchen. Then Duke started barking. "Quiet, Duke!" Gwen said. "They'll think this place is a madhouse!"

Mia sat quietly with Socks as the front door opened and Gwen greeted her family. There was a babble of voices, and Socks's ears twitched nervously.

"It's fine," Mia soothed him.

"Are you sure you're OK, darling?" a woman said.

"Of course she'll be OK, she's with me," Gwen said firmly. "And we're going to have a lovely afternoon. The girl from next door is here too, so she'll have someone to play with."

The front door closed and Gwen's voice got closer. "Mia," she called, "come and meet my granddaughter!"

"See you in a minute, Socks," Mia said, scrambling to her feet.

She went to the door and into the lounge. Then her mouth fell open in shock. There, with Gwen's arm around her, her hair in a perfect ponytail and wearing a glittery pink dress – was Zara!

7

Zara was Gwen's granddaughter!

"Oh!" was all Mia could say.

"Hi, Mia," Zara said.

Gwen looked from one girl to the other. "Do you know each other?"

"We're in the same class, Granny," Zara mumbled, looking at her feet.

"Brilliant!" Gwen said. "Well, you girls sit and chat while I get my cake out of the oven, and then we can show you Socks. He's the special animal I was telling you about."

She planted a kiss on Zara's head, then bustled away, making Duke start barking again.

As the noise faded away, Mia looked at Zara crossly. She'd stolen Emily and lied about tripping her up, and now she was going to take Gwen and Socks too!

"I didn't know you knew my grandma," Zara said. She sat down next to Sally, who was curled up on the sofa, and gently stroked her ears.

"I live next door," Mia told her, sitting on the other side of Sally and stroking her too. "I've been helping at the wildlife centre."

"This is such a cool house," Zara said, looking around at the plants and the animals. Duke was sprawled out on the rug, panting happily, and Tabs was resting in her favourite place on the back of Gwen's chair. "It's like something out of a story."

"Haven't you been here before?" Mia asked. She'd been to *her* grandparents' house a hundred times.

Zara nodded. "But not very often," she said.

"But you live close now, you can come here all the time," Mia said, trying not to think about how Zara moving had ruined things with her and Emily.

"Yes." Zara tickled Sally and she stretched out happily.

Traitor, Mia thought, *you're meant to be my friend!*

"So, who's Socks?" Zara asked, looking around the room. Mia heard a familiar yipping from the conservatory.

"He's not a pet," she told Zara, "he's a wild animal, so you can't stroke him, OK?"

Zara nodded, her eyes wide. "What is he?" she whispered.

Mia opened the conservatory door and walked in.

Zara gasped and Mia couldn't help feeling proud. It was nice to be able to show off to Zara, for once!

"He's so cute!" Zara exclaimed.

"We've been looking after him," Mia explained. "He's not really ours, because he's wild, but he feels like he is a little bit."

Gwen came in and put her arms around them both. "What do you think to my surprise?" she asked Zara.

"He's so cool, Granny!" Zara couldn't take her eyes off Socks.

"Let's go and get some banana bread before Duke eats it all." Gwen said. "And it's nearly ice cream o'clock."

"Yay, ice cream o'clock! Thanks, Granny." Zara hugged Gwen around her middle.

When Gwen went to get the food, Zara knelt down next to Mia in front of Socks's cage.

"Sorry about tripping you up," she said, winding her hair around her finger awkwardly. "It was an accident, I promise,

but then I didn't want Emily to know so I . . .
I lied about it. I'm sorry."

Mia was really surprised. Zara was being
so nice. For a second she thought it was
some kind of trick, but Zara was looking
at her anxiously, her eyes wide. She looked
like she really was sorry.

"It's OK," Mia told her.

To her surprise, Zara flung her arms
around her and gave her such a big hug that
they almost toppled over.

"Whoa!" Mia said as they wobbled
upright. Both girls burst out laughing.

Socks scampered up and down, then he
gave a bark like he was laughing too.

🐾

The next day, Mia had to go back to school,
but now she and Zara had made friends, she
wasn't dreading it. In fact, she was looking
forward to seeing her friends and telling

them all about Socks and the wildlife sanctuary.

When she got to the playground, Emily and Zara were standing together. Zara grinned as she saw her and raced over. Emily followed behind.

Zara slipped her arm into Mia's as they walked around the playground. "I'm going to Granny's again after school to see Socks; are you coming?" she said.

Mia nodded happily. "The vet's going to look at his leg again today," she said. "And then I'm going to the wildlife centre at the weekend. There's a lovely cat there. I call him Boots, because he's got patches on his paws too."

"I'm going to see Granny and Socks on Saturday," Zara said. "You should come round, we can walk Duke. Mum said she'd pick me up after lunch – but I said I had to stay until after three o'clock!"

"What happens at three o'clock?" Emily asked, sounding confused.

But Mia and Zara were already laughing. The bell went and they started walking back into school.

As they walked, Emily lagged behind. Mia glanced back at her friend, then looked at herself and Zara, arm in arm, and suddenly realized that they were leaving Emily out. She remembered how that felt.

"Can Emily come to meet Socks, too?" she asked. "We can ask Aunty Gwen."

"Sure, Granny won't mind!" Zara said.

Emily's face brightened.

Mia held out her other arm and Emily took it, giving her a squeeze. All three girls walked into class together.

🐾

The next three weeks passed so quickly. School was much better now that Mia was friends with Emily *and* Zara. She could hardly remember how upset she'd been. She went round to visit Gwen and Socks almost every day, and Zara visited lots too. Socks had been moved into a bigger pen in the garden, so there was more room for him to run around.

"You know he'll have to go back into the wild soon," Gwen said nearly every time they saw him. Mia always nodded. She was glad he was better, but she wished he could stay.

Gwen was waiting when Zara and Mia arrived one day. "I have good news," she said, as Duke jumped up to lick them hello.

"Did the vet say Socks was getting better?" Mia asked.

"Come and see." Gwen grinned.

They rushed into the conservatory and out into the garden. Socks was still in his pen, but the cast was gone!

His poorly leg looked a bit skinnier than the others, and he was licking it carefully.

"The vet said that we've been taking really good care of him," Gwen said. "As soon as he gets the strength back in his leg, we can release him."

"When?" Mia asked, a horrible sinking feeling in her tummy.

"We'll see how he's doing at the weekend," Gwen said. Mia nodded.

Socks tumbled over in his cage, pawing at the bars. Zara giggled at his antics, but Mia couldn't. Two days and then she'd never see Socks again.

♥ ✤ ★ ✿ **8** ✿ ★ ✤ ♥

"This is so exciting!" Emily squealed as Mia and Gwen pulled up at the wildlife sanctuary. Gwen had said it was OK for all three girls to help out, as long as everyone listened to her and Mandy. They were going to have the morning there, and then that night they were going to have a party, with Zara's family and Mia's parents too, to release Socks back into the wild.

"This is where you put your coats," Mia said, taking the others into the staffroom. "And this is where all the animals are!"

She led them into the main room. There were fewer animals there now as the weather was getting warmer and lots of the animals that had been staying for the winter had been released.

"This is Nutkin and this is Ted," Mia showed Zara two squirrels. "We feed them walnuts, hazelnuts and mixed fruit."

"Sometimes a little human nibbles on the squirrel food too," Gwen said, giving Mia a squeeze.

"It's so tasty!" Mia laughed.

"This is so cool!" Zara said. Emily nodded. Mia felt really proud as she showed them around. And she felt even prouder when Mandy came to meet them.

"Mia is one of our best volunteers," she told them. "She's been such a big help these last few weeks. Everyone loves her – and someone in particular..."

"Oh, yes, show them Boots," Gwen said.

Mia went over to the pen right in the corner.

"Here he is," she said.

As soon as he saw Mia, Boots came right up to the bars, rubbing his face on the mesh and meowing excitedly.

"Can I take him out?" Mia asked.

"Check that Duke's out of the way," Gwen said.

"I'll find him," Zara volunteered. She disappeared and came back a minute later, giggling. "He's asleep on the staffroom sofa," she laughed.

Gwen rolled her eyes. With the staffroom door safely shut, Mia opened Boots's pen.

Boots burst out and rushed up to her, rubbing his body around her ankles. "Hello!" Mia bent down to stroke him, and he bumped her forehead with his.

"He's never that friendly with anyone else," Mandy said admiringly. "You've done brilliantly with him, Mia."

"He's so lovely!" Emily said. She and Zara knelt down and tried to tempt Boots over, but he stuck by Mia's side.

Mia trailed her fingers though his silky fur as he snuggled close to her. He turned, his big blue eyes bright, and nuzzled his head into her hand, as if he was asking for more strokes. He had completely recovered from the cat flu, and he was different to the scared cat he'd been when he first arrived. He'd put on some weight while he was at the centre, and his ginger coat was glossy and smooth. The only thing that was the same were the four white markings on his legs.

While Mandy showed Zara and Emily how to clean out the pen, Mia played with Boots happily.

"He's so much better." Gwen came over and tickled him behind the ears. "We'll be looking for a new home for him soon as well."

"Really?" Mia asked. She bent down and concentrated on stroking Boots so no one would see she was upset. First she was losing Socks, now Boots was going too.

"It's always hard to let animals go. I wish I could keep them all myself," Gwen said. "But it's so great that he'll be able to have a happy home now. And, sadly, there are always new animals that need our help."

But they're not Boots, Mia thought to herself.

The phone rang and Gwen bustled off to answer it.

Boots put his front paws on Mia's leg and stood up to peer at her. Then he jumped into her lap for a cuddle. Mia stroked him sadly.

She glanced up and saw Zara watching her curiously.

Mia tried to be happy that Socks and Boots were both better, but she couldn't help thinking about how miserable she'd been and how good everything had been since she'd met them. She was going to miss them both so much.

"Has everyone got a drink?" Gwen called out.

Mia looked round the room. Her mum and dad were there, holding champagne flutes full of celebratory bubbly wine. Mandy from the wildlife sanctuary and Zara's parents were there too. Gwen looked so happy to see them. She kept putting her arm around her son and had even hugged Zara's mum earlier. Duke was rushing around everyone's legs, but Zara's mum didn't seem to mind. In fact, Mia even saw her pat him on the head when she thought no one was looking.

Zara and Emily were there too. Gwen

had got fizzy drinks for them, but let them have it in the posh champagne glasses.

Gwen nodded out to the garden, where Socks's pen was. It was starting to get dark, and Socks was alert, running up and down his pen and sniffing the air, looking at the back of the garden intently.

Gwen clinked a spoon against her glass to get everyone's attention. "We're here to say goodbye to Socks," she said. "It's been a privilege to meet such a lovely fox. And through him, I've made a new friend, Mia." Gwen smiled at her, her blue eyes crinkling. "And I've spent lots of time with my lovely granddaughter, Zara. Now I'm here with all my family, it's time we send Socks home to his. Mia, shall we do the honours?"

Mia nodded. Mum squeezed her hand as she and Gwen went outside.

It was just getting dark, and everything

in the garden was a blue-grey. Light was spilling out from the conservatory, but the doors shut off all the noise of the party.

Socks was prowling up and down in his pen, looking bright eyed as he sniffed the air.

"Hi, Socks," Mia said quietly.

He kept staring at the back of the garden.

"Are your family out there?" Mia asked him.

She looked back to the conservatory, where her family and friends were waiting. They'd turned off the lights so that they could see out into the garden better.

"I'll miss you," Mia said. She looked at Gwen and she nodded. Gwen opened the pen door.

Socks took a step forward, then ran straight out and disappeared into the bushes.

There was a rustle of leaves, and a few happy yips, and he was gone.

Mia strained her eyes into the darkness, but there was no sign of him. He'd disappeared.

"Is that it?" she asked. She felt so disappointed.

Gwen put her arm around Mia's shoulders and gave a gentle laugh. "He's back where he belongs."

They went back inside. Everyone was cheerful. "He ran like a rocket!" Dad grinned. "His leg must be completely better. You did a brilliant job looking after him, Mia."

Mia nodded, trying not to cry. She knew he was wild, but she hadn't expected Socks to just run away like that.

Emily and Zara came over "Are you OK?" Emily asked.

Mia nodded. "I knew I couldn't keep him for ever. He's not a pet. I just wish..." She stopped as a sob caught in her throat. "I just wish he'd said goodbye..."

Mum was singing in the kitchen when Mia came down for breakfast the next day.

"I'm going to need your help today," she told Mia happily.

"Can I go to the wildlife sanctuary?" Mia said.

"If you spend any more time there they're going to give you your own pen," Dad joked.

"Not today!" Mum said cheerfully. "I need you to go and tidy your bedroom. I don't want any little things on the floor."

Mia groaned. "It's tidy!" she said.

"Well, go and make it *super* tidy!" Mum replied.

Mia shut the kitchen door crossly. As she did, Jamie ran in from the back garden excitedly. "Was that the front door?" he asked.

"No," Mia replied. Why were her family being so strange today?

She went upstairs and started tidying up grumpily.

After a while Mum came up and nodded approvingly. "It'll be worth it, you'll see!" she said. Then she disappeared downstairs again.

Mia had just finished tidying when the doorbell rang.

"Mia, it's for you!" Mum called.

"Quick!" Dad yelled.

Mia rushed downstairs. Mum, Dad and Jamie were all standing around the door, nudging one another and smiling expectantly.

"Open it!" Mum said.

Mia opened the door. There, on the doorstep, were Gwen and Zara. For once Duke wasn't with them, but Gwen was holding an animal carrier.

"What's that?" Mia asked curiously.

"Bring him through to the lounge," Mum said.

"It was all Zara's idea," Gwen said, as she followed Mum though, carrying the animal box. She put it down on the floor gently. "We couldn't keep Socks, that wouldn't be right. He's a wild animal. But Zara pointed out that there was another animal that loves you very much, one that really needed a home..."

Mia looked at her family, who were all grinning like loons. Zara and Gwen were wreathed in smiles too. Then she bent down and looked in the animal carrier. Inside was Boots!

He was curled up at the back, but he looked up when he saw Mia, and came to the front of the carrier. Mia put her fingers up to the wire and let him sniff them. "Meow," he said.

Dad bent down next to her and started undoing the carrier. "He's yours," he said.

"You've done such a good job caring for the animals, you really deserve one of your own."

"But you said no," Mia gasped, looking from her mum to her dad in disbelief. "You always say no."

Mum gave me a smile. "You've proved you can be a responsible pet owner," she said. "Besides, from what we hear, he really loves you."

"I love him," Mia said. It still didn't feel real. Boots was here, in her house. And he was going to stay, for ever. Dad opened the door and he came out cautiously. He padded over to her, sniffing around everything, and Mia ran her hand over his soft fur. "It's OK, Boots," she said. "You're safe here."

Mia started half-laughing, half-crying, as Boots climbed into her lap for a cuddle. "You don't have to be scared ever again," she told him, reaching down to kiss him on the top of his furry head.

Mia looked up at Zara and Gwen. "You did this?" she asked Zara.

Zara gave a smile and a shrug. "It was at the party last night," she said as she bent down to stroke Boots. "I just said, why doesn't Mia have Boots."

"And I said, that's a very good question!" Gwen laughed. "I spoke to your parents, and they agreed. We normally do house visits to check the people who adopt our animals, but we thought we could skip that this time."

"I can't believe you said yes!" Mia looked up at her mum.

"You looked so sad when Socks left!" Mum said. "But you have to look after him, and make sure there aren't little things lying around that he can eat. This isn't something that will last for just six weeks, he's going to be part of the family for years and years."

Mia's heart gave a little happy jump at the thought. "I will look after him," she promised. She looked at the little cat curled up in her arms. He was watching everything, his big blue eyes wide, but he didn't seem too scared. Mia stroked his head and felt him start to purr.

"And you can't adopt every animal that you meet at the shelter," Gwen said, her blue eyes twinkling. "I assume that you'll keep coming to help us out?"

"Of course!" Mia said. "And you'll come too, won't you, Zara?"

Zara nodded. "I'm going to spend every Saturday with Granny now!" Gwen beamed with delight.

"We can invite Emily too," Gwen said. "The more helpers the better."

"We have to invite her to come and play with Boots!" Mia said.

"When he's settled in a bit," Mum nodded.

"He's great," Jamie said, reaching out to stroke him.

"You can share him too," Mia told her brother, generously.

"Nah!" Jaime said. "Now we're allowed animals, I'm getting a pit bull!"

"No you're not!" Dad laughed.

"Do they have any pit bulls at the wildlife centre, Gwen?" Jamie asked.

"I'll let you know if we get any," Gwen said, her eyes twinkling.

"Oh, no you won't!" Mum said. "One cat is enough."

"Pit bulls are very sweet natured..." Gwen told her.

Mia grinned as her family chatted. In her arms, Boots snuggled up happily.

He was hers, and he was never leaving.

"Time for bed," Mum said later that night. "Boots will still be here in the morning."

Mia hugged Mum and Dad goodnight, then went over to stroke Boots. They'd spent the whole day settling him in and showing him all the new things they'd got to make their house feel like his for ever home. He was snuggled in his basket in the corner of the living room, looking like he'd always been there.

She bent down and stroked his head, and he flipped over so she could tickle his tummy.

"Goodnight," she said, reaching down to kiss him.

Mia went upstairs, called goodnight to Jamie, then went into her room. It was still a little bit light, so she pulled her curtains tightly shut and jumped into bed.

She'd just got in when there was a padding sound and Boots jumped up on to the bed. "Boots," Mia giggled, "you've got your own bed downstairs!"

Boots started purring loudly and she stroked his back. She couldn't believe he was really hers. He turned in a circle, then curled up next to her. Mia stroked him gently as she shut her eyes and thought about Socks. It was thanks to him that she'd made friends with Gwen, and gone to the wildlife centre, and met Boots. The fox cub might be gone, but she had a piece of him for ever.

Just then she heard a familiar yipping noise outside. Mia's eyes shot open. She looked at Boots, whose ears were twitching. "Did you hear that?" Mia asked. Boots blinked as if he was saying yes.

Mia scrambled up and put her head under her curtains. There, in the purply twilight, was a fox – a familiar fox with four black socks on his feet.

"Socks!" Mia breathed.

Boots scrambled around and sat on the windowsill next to her, purring happily.

Mia stroked him gently as she looked down at her fox. "Thank you, Socks," she said.

He gave one last yip, seeming to smile at her, then he disappeared, off to live his wild life.

Mia snuggled down with her cat happily. Socks had come to say goodbye, after all.

Fox
Care Tips!

The Riverside Animal Centre

Thank you to the Riverside Animal Centre, who answered all my questions about rescuing animals and returning them to the wild. Any mistakes in this book are my fault, not theirs.

The Riverside Animal Centre is based in Beddington Park, within the London Borough of Sutton. They provide a hospital and rehabilitation service for all species of British wild mammals and birds, ranging from foxes, badgers and deer through to pigeons, corvids like ravens and crows, and songbirds.

In addition to their core wildlife work, they also have a small cat rescue unit, which works to help cats in immediate need in our local area. They are always looking for new homes for their cats.

The centre is completely dependent on donations to help foxes like Socks, hares like Flopsy, Mopsy and Cottontail, and cats like Boots.

If you want to help, go to
www.londonwildcaretrust.co.uk
to make a donation, or send a cheque to the Riverside Animal Centre,
Beddington Park, Church Road,
Wallington, SM6 7NN.
Registered Charity, number 1087273.

Wildlife Watching

Mia and Gwen are lucky enough to watch foxes playing in their gardens.

Here are some top tips for watching foxes in the wild:

- Go out at dusk. Adult foxes are mainly nocturnal, which means they mainly come out at night. The best time to see them is in the evening as it's getting dark, when they're just waking up! Baby fox cubs like Socks and his family often come out and play in the afternoon if their mum thinks it's safe, but you have to be very lucky to spot them.

- Wear the right clothes. Try and choose colours that blend in with the surroundings, and make sure you're not wearing clothes that rustle or make too much noise when you move.

- Identify the best spot – where you know the foxes live. See if your town has any local wildlife clubs that do wildlife watching, or know where the best spots are.

- Sit downwind. Foxes have a very good sense of smell. If they smell you, they might not come out at all. So make sure you're sitting with the wind blowing into your face, so that your smell is being carried away from the animals.
- Sit quietly. Get into a comfortable position and sit as quietly as you can.
- Put some of their favourite food out. Make sure you check what food is safe for them to eat, and put some in a clearing near their den. It might tempt them out!
- Watch a documentary! Don't be disappointed if you don't see the foxes. At least there are lots of brilliant wildlife documentaries where you can learn about all kind of animals.

Wildlife In Your Garden

You can still help animals even if you can't volunteer in a wildlife sanctuary like Mia, Emily and Zara. People's houses have taken over a lot of land that animals used to live on, so every bit of wildness helps. Why not make a bit of your garden into a wildlife wilderness? Make sure you ask a parent or guardian first!

- You could build habitats for insects, small mammals and even amphibians by piling up some logs of wood.
- Leave a little patch at the end of your garden to grow wild to encourage different insects and small animals.
- Put up bird feeders and bird nesting boxes. If a bird family does move into your nesting box, it might come back every year!
- If you have a cat, make sure that it wears a collar with a bell so that it doesn't hurt the local birds.

- Cut a small hole in your garden fences – no bigger than a book – to let hedgehogs though.
- Encourage bees by planting plants that have lots of pollen.
- Don't tidy your garden too much! In autumn, leave piles of fallen leaves for insects to live in.
- To attract hedgehogs, make a tepee style pile (always check for hedgehogs before lighting a bonfire).
- Lastly, if you wanted to, your family could build a pond. Ponds are great for encouraging all kinds of creatures to visit your garden, but make sure it has shallow sides for frogs and newts to come in.

From tiny changes like building a log pile or putting up a birdhouse to big changes like making a pond, every little thing helps make a home for wildlife in our gardens – and you can have fun watching them!

Fox Facts

- A fox's house is called a den.
- Male foxes are called a dog, females are called vixens, and babies are cubs.
- Foxes are actually part of the dog family, the same family as wolves. Foxes are the only member of the dog family that can retract their claws like cats can.
- Foxes have great night vision, sharp hearing and a keen sense of smell. They see, hear and smell you long before you see them!
- Foxes have whiskers on their legs as well as their faces, which help them find their way around.
- Foxes don't chew their food, they use special teeth at the back of their mouths to tear it into small chunks.
- Foxes are incredibly successful animals because they'll eat almost anything. They have evolved to live in urban areas as well as the countryside.

- A fox's tail is called a brush.
- Foxes use up to 28 different calls to talk to each other!
- Foxes used to be hunted for fun. Luckily, this was made illegal in Scotland in 2002, and in England and Wales in 2004.
- Foxes are native to Europe, Asia and North Africa, but they also live in Australia now, having been taken there by people a long time ago.
- There are lots of different types of fox. The foxes we have in the UK are Red foxes, but there are also Arctic foxes, Fennec foxes and Gray foxes. They all look quite different to Socks and his family!

Look out for more adorable books

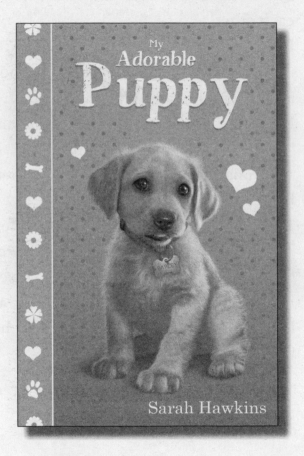